Another Sommer-Time Story

Can You Help Me Find My Smile?

By Carl Sommer
Illustrated by Greg Budwine

Advance • HOUSTON
PUBLISHING, INC.

Permissions
Advance Publishing, Inc.
6950 Fulton St.
Houston, TX 77022

http://www.advancepublishing.com

First Edition
Printed in Singapore

Library of Congress Cataloging-in-Publication Data

Sommer, Carl, 1930-
    Can you help me find my smile? / by Carl Sommer ; illustrated by Greg Budwine. – 1st ed.
      p. cm. – (Another Sommer-time story)
    Summary: Teddy, a bear who is constantly grumpy, discovers that the secret to being happy is helping others.
    ISBN 1-57537-007-7 (hc : alk. paper). – ISBN 1-57537-055-7 (lib. bdg. : alk. paper)
    [1. Bears–Fiction. 2. Happiness–Fiction. 3. Conduct of life–Fiction.] I. Budwine, Greg, ill. II. Title. III. Series: Sommer, Carl, 1930- Another Sommer-time story.
PZ7.S696235Can 1997
[E]–dc20   96-24345
                                                     CIP
                                                     AC

Can You Help Me Find My Smile?

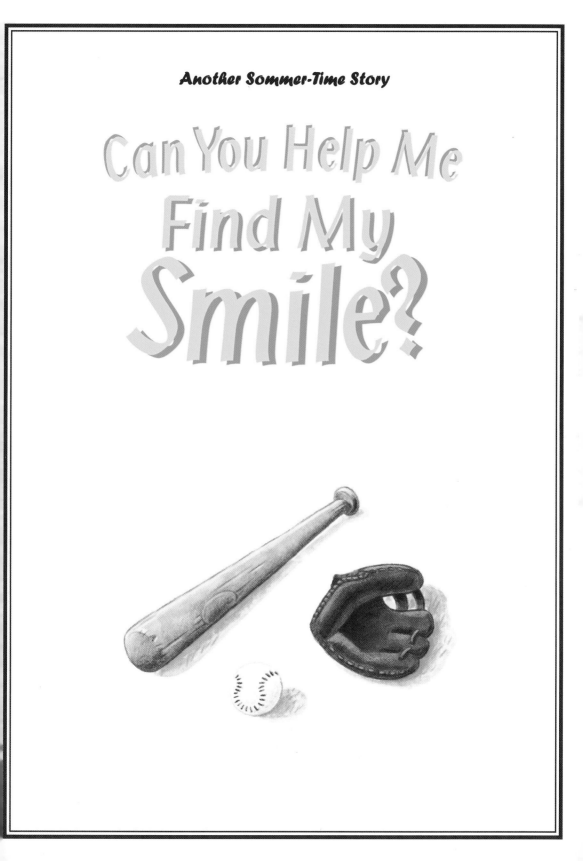

Once there was a young bear named Teddy who lived with his dad, mom, and sister, Susie.

Teddy was a very happy baby—he always smiled.

But as Teddy grew older, he began to lose his smile. That made him feel grumpy.

Dad and Mom loved Teddy and did many nice things for him. They gave him gifts for special times, played games with him, and took him on fishing trips.

Still Teddy felt grumpy—he hardly ever smiled.

Teddy did not like being grumpy. "If I just had a new bat and ball," he thought, "I know I'd get my smile back."

Sure enough, when he got a new bat and ball, Teddy smiled.

He was smiling when it was his turn to bat...

...but he quit smiling when it was his turn to play in the outfield. Grumpy Teddy did not like running after the ball. He only wanted to hit the ball.

"Playing ball isn't much fun after all," grumbled Teddy.

Teddy's dad and mom gave him a new bicycle for his birthday.

"Hooray!" shouted Teddy. "This bike will surely bring back my smile!"

Dad and Mom took him to the park, and happy Teddy had great fun riding down the hill...

. . . but unhappy Teddy grumbled when he had to pedal back up the hill.

Before long, riding his bike did not make him smile anymore.

It seemed everything Teddy did only made him happy for a short while. Teddy became a very grumpy bear—now he never smiled.

Teddy wanted so much to be happy. One day he told a friend, "I don't like being so grumpy. Can you help me find my smile?"

"Sure!" said his friend. "We'll go to Playland. You'll find your smile there!"

Off they went. Teddy and his friend rode all kinds of rides. Teddy tried very hard to find his smile at Playland.

But the more rides he rode, the grumpier he became.

The following day Teddy asked another friend, "Can you help me find my smile?"

"I sure can!" answered his friend. "I know just what to do. Let's go swimming in the river. You'll find plenty of smiles there!"

Everyone was happy and had fun swimming, except Teddy. He just laid on his float with a big frown on his face.

Sometime later Teddy told an older friend, "I've tried very hard to find my smile, but nothing works. Maybe I can ask my grandpa what to do."

His friend shook his head and laughed. "Grandpas can't help kids. They're too old!"

"Well," Teddy asked, "do *you* know where my smile is?"

"Of course! Your smile is inside you! Just keep telling yourself that you're happy, and then put a big smile on your face."

Teddy did just what his friend said. He went home and stood in front of a mirror.

"I am happy!" he said.

"I am very happy!

"I am really very happy!" Then he grinned as big as he could.

But it was not a real smile, and it did not make him happy. In fact, it made him even grumpier.

One day Teddy's family went to visit Grandpa and Grandma. They lived on a farm with many kinds of animals.

"Maybe I can do something on the farm that will make me happy," thought Teddy. "I can feed the animals and play with them. That should make me smile!"

Teddy and Susie fed the ducks and chickens.
Susie had lots of fun and lots of smiles. But
not Teddy—he never smiled.

Teddy and Susie fed the goats and rode the horses.

Susie had lots of fun and lots of smiles. But not Teddy—he never smiled.

Nothing Teddy did on the farm made him smile. Now he was grumpier than ever.

Teddy went to Grandpa who was sitting in his rocking chair. Grandpa lifted Teddy onto his lap. Then he gave him a great big hug. Grandpa loved Teddy.

"Teddy," asked Grandpa, "where is your smile?"

"I don't know," answered Teddy.

"Maybe I can help you find it," said Grandpa.

Teddy shook his head. "I don't think so. My friend says, 'Grandpas can't help kids. They're too old.'"

Grandpa laughed a big laugh. Then he asked, "Did your friend help you find your smile?"

"No," said Teddy softly. Suddenly he thought, "All my friends have been wrong. Maybe Grandpa *can* help me!"

Teddy lowered his head and whispered, "Grandpa, can you help me find my smile?"

Grandpa stopped rocking. He gently lifted Teddy's head.

"When you try to make only *yourself* happy," said Grandpa, "you will always be sad and grumpy. But when you try to make *others* happy, you will find your smile."

"That doesn't seem right, Grandpa," said Teddy. "If I stop trying to make myself happy, then I'll *really* be sad!"

"No, no," said Grandpa as he patted Teddy's head. "Come with me."

"Where are we going?" asked Teddy.

"You'll see," answered Grandpa. They climbed into Grandpa's car and off they went.

As they drove around the town, Grandpa said, "Look Teddy. Everywhere you go there are those who are poor and needy. If you help those who really need help, you will find your smile."

"I don't understand, Grandpa," said Teddy, shaking his head. "But I'm going to do just as you say. I'm going to try real hard to make others happy."

Soon it was time for Teddy and his family to leave the farm. They packed their bags and waved goodbye to Grandpa and Grandma.

On the way home, Teddy thought and thought about what Grandpa had said. He began thinking about others instead of himself. He wondered, "How can I make someone else happy?"

Finally, he got an idea!

The next morning, Teddy woke up early. He was ready to get started.

First he made his bed, then he put all his clothes and toys away. He had decided to clean the whole room! "This will surely make Mom happy," Teddy said to himself.

While cleaning his room, Teddy thought about how surprised and happy Mom would be.

The more he thought about making Mom happy, the less grumpy he felt.

Teddy did not know it, but as he cleaned his room ... he began to smile.

In school Teddy sat in front of a boy named Billy. Billy often hid Teddy's books just to make him mad.

Sometimes he even tried to get Teddy in trouble with the teacher.

But this time *Billy* was in trouble—he had lost his notebook. And he did not want to tell the teacher that his mother did not have the money to buy another one.

Teddy remembered what Grandpa had told him about making *others* happy. Teddy knew Billy was poor, so he turned around and said, "Billy, you can have my extra notebook."

Billy was so happy. "Thank you, Teddy!"

Teddy did not know it, but he had a smile on his face. And he had a new friend—Billy.

While walking home from school, Teddy saw a friend having trouble carrying her books.

"Bonnie!" called Teddy. "Let me help you."

"Thank you," she said.

Teddy felt very happy as he carried Bonnie's books. He did not know it, but he had a big smile on his face.

That afternoon Mom went into Teddy's bedroom.

Was she ever surprised! "Who cleaned up this room?"

There stood Teddy with the biggest smile on his face. "I did, Mom!"

"I'm so happy!" said his mother. Then she gave Teddy a great big hug.

That night Teddy felt so good—he had made his mom happy.

Now he wanted to make his dad happy. But what could he do?

"The garden!" thought Teddy. "Tomorrow I'm supposed to help Dad pull weeds from the garden. I'll do it all by myself! Will he ever be surprised . . . and happy!"

The next afternoon while his friends played, Teddy went to work in the garden. He pulled out all the weeds by himself. He even did extra work—he raked the yard!

It was hard work, but Teddy was happy thinking about how glad Dad would be when he saw the garden and the yard.

Teddy did not know it, but while working he had a great big smile on his face.

When Dad got home from work that day, he was so surprised! "Who has been working in the garden, and...who raked the yard?" Dad could not believe his eyes.

There stood Teddy with the biggest smile ever. "I did, Dad!"

Dad picked Teddy up and gave him a great big hug. Finally, Teddy realized...he was happy! He had found his smile by helping others!

When Teddy went back to the farm, he ran to
Grandpa and jumped onto his lap. With a great
big smile he said, "It works, Grandpa! It works!"
"What works?" asked Grandpa.

"Remember? You said if I wanted to find my smile, I must help others."

"That's right," nodded Grandpa.

"Well," said Teddy, "I began making others happy, and now I have the biggest smile in the whole world!"

From then on wherever Teddy went, he led the way by making others happy.

No longer was Teddy a grumpy bear. Now he had lots of smiles. His friends even gave him a new name—Smiley Bear.

Best of all Teddy never forgot Grandpa's lesson: Happiness comes by helping others.